For Mom and Dad.

Published in 2016 by Simply Read Books | www.simplyreadbooks.com
Text & Illustrations © 2016 Emily Dove

LIBRARY AND ARCHIVES CANADA CATALOGUING IN PUBLICATION

Dove, Emily, 1985-, author, illustrator
Wendell the narwhal / written and illustrated by
Emily Dove.
ISBN 978-1-927018-66-8 (bound)
1. Narwhal--Juvenile fiction. I. Title.
PZ7.1.D68We 2015   C813'.6   C2014-906177-3

We gratefully acknowledge for their financial support of our publishing program the Canada Council for the Arts, the BC Arts Council, and the Government of Canada through the Canada Book Fund (CBF).

Manufactured in South Korea.
Book design by Emily Dove and Heather Lohnes.
This book is typeset in Mr. Eaves, created by Zuzana Licko for Emigre typefoundry.
10 9 8 7 6 5

Wendell

the
NARWHAL

emily dove

SIMPLY READ BOOKS

Wendell the narwhal
just wants to make music.

There's only one problem.

He can't.

All the other animals make music.

POP POP
POP POP
POP POP
POP POP

sigh.

The
jellyfish
go...

WUBBA

WUB

WUB

POP WUB POP
WUB WUB WUB
POP
WUB POP
POP WUB
POP WUB
POP WUB
POP WUB POP
WUB POP
POP WUB POP

The
blowfish
goes…

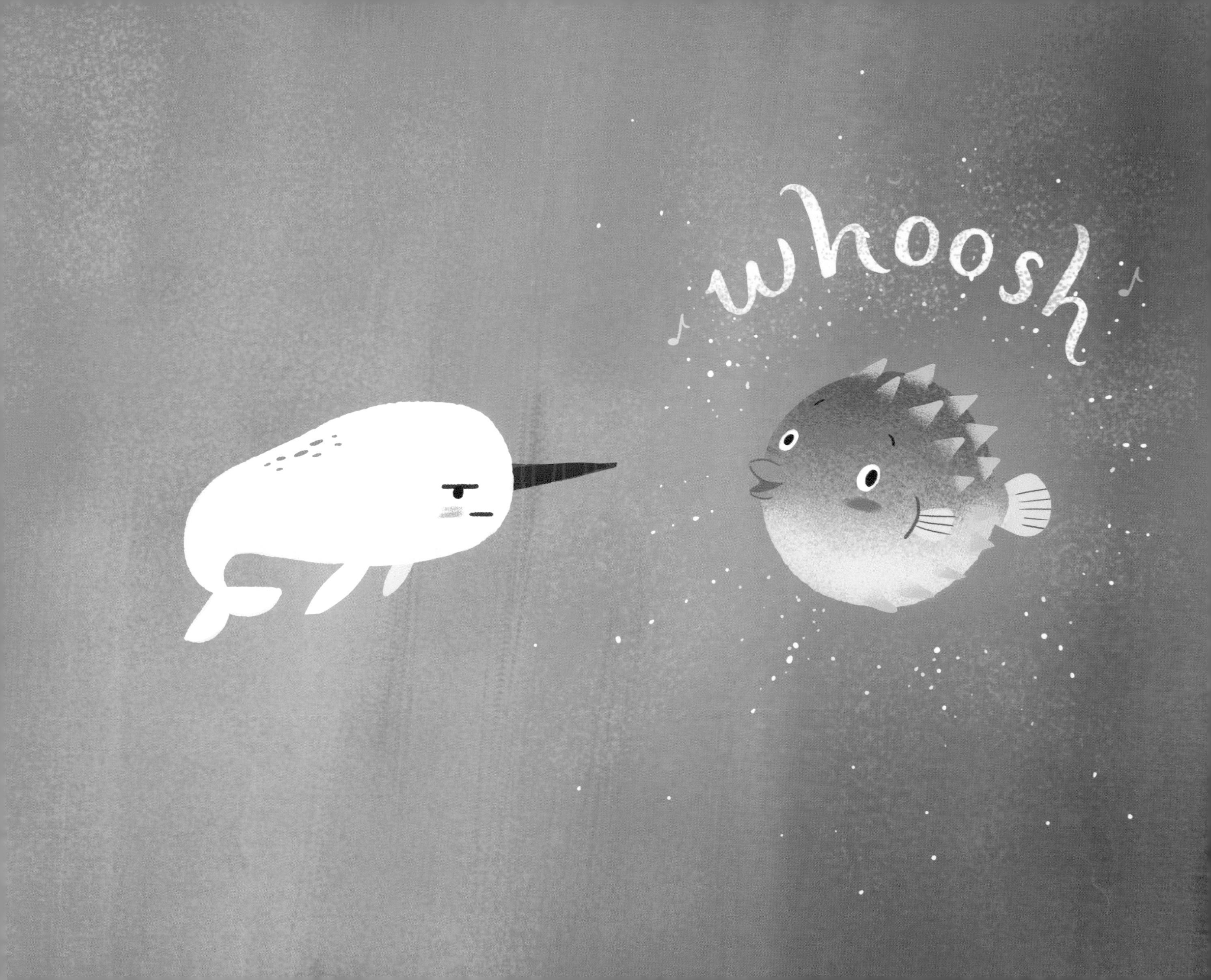
whoosh

POP WUB
WHOOSH POP
WUB WUB
POP
WUB
POP
WHOOSH POP
POP WUB POP POP
WHOOSH
WUB
POP
POP
WUB
POP
WUB
WHOOSH POP
POP
WUB
POP WUB
WHOOSH
WHOOSH
WUB
POP
WHOOSH

TWEEDLY dee
WUB
WUB
WUB
WUB
WHOOSH
WUB
POP
POP
WUB
WHOOSH
TWEEDLY dee
WUB
WEEDLy dee
POP
WHOOSH
POP
TWEEDLY dee
POP
POP
WUB WUB
WHOOSH
WUB
POP
TWEEDLy dee
TWEEDLY dee
WHOOSH
POP
WHOOSH
WUB
WUB
POP
WUB
WUB
POP
TWEEDLy dee
WUB
WUB
POP

And the
clam goes...

CLAPPY

♫ CLAP ♪

CLAP!

Now the ocean is too

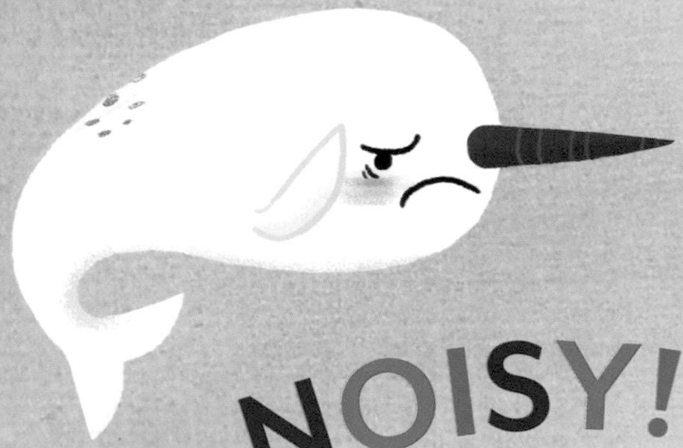

NOISY!

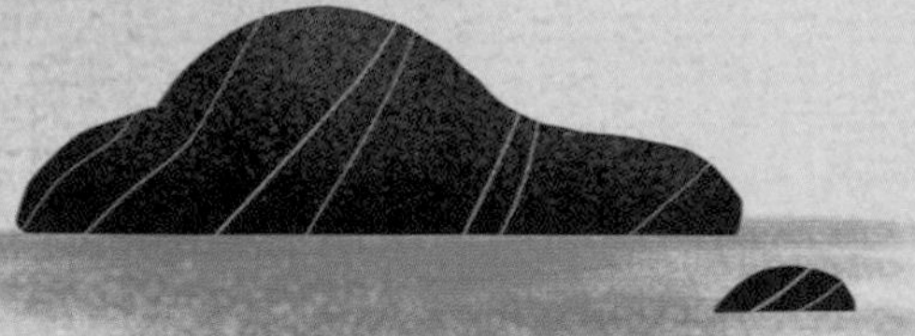

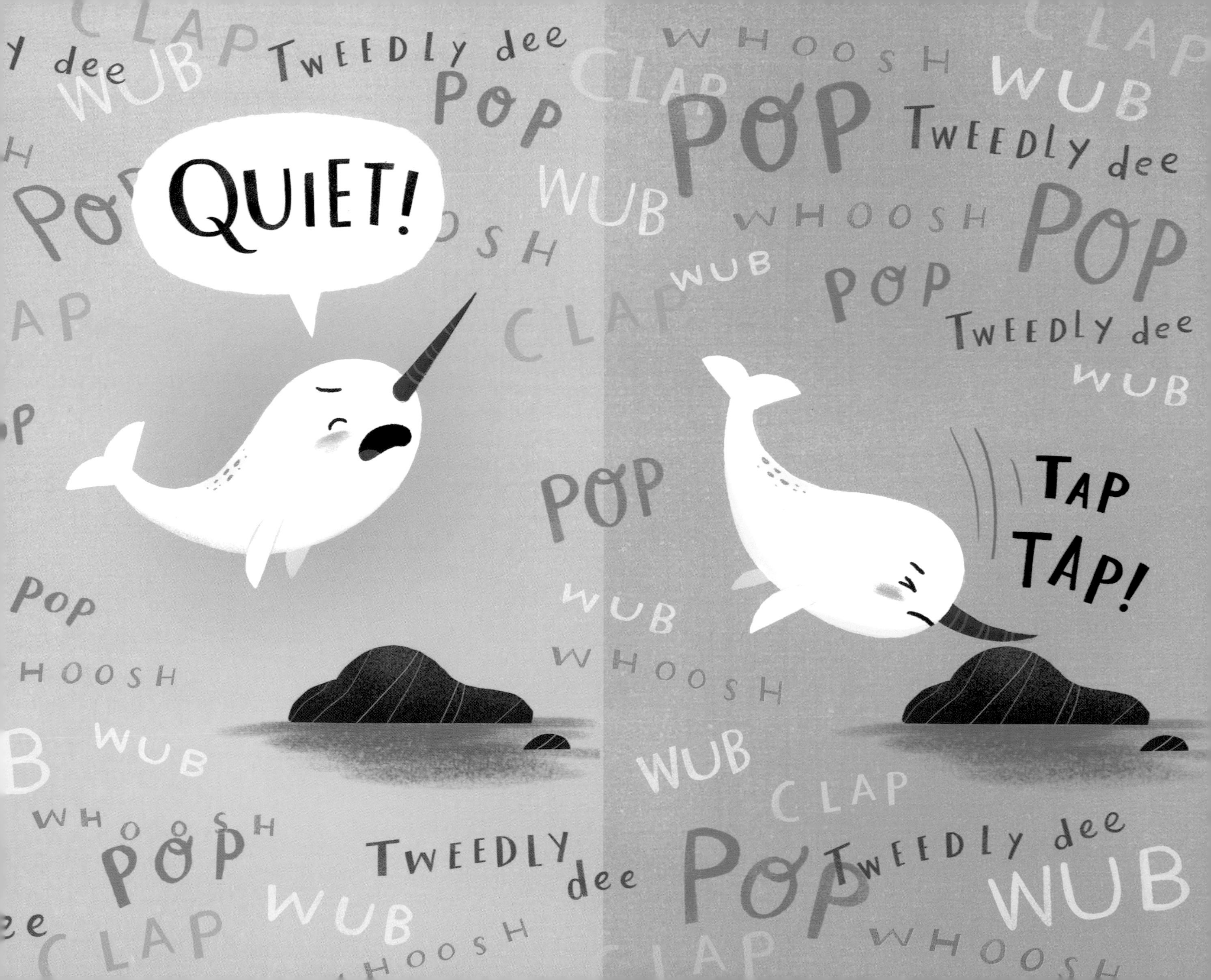
QUIET!
TAP
TAP!

phew.

Now the ocean is too…

...quiet.

So Wendell does.

The octopus goes…

The jellyfish go…

The blowfish goes…

The whale goes...

T<small>WEEDLY</small>
dee

And the clam
goes...

C<small>LAPPY</small>
C<small>LAP</small>
C<small>LAP</small>!

Now the ocean is
not too noisy
and not too quiet.

TWEEE

POP whoosh PO

CLAPPY CLAP

WUB WUB WUB

It is marvelously musical.